This book belongs to:

_____

_____

_____

Gregory the Spider

Romping through the Year

by Cynthia Dreeman Meyer   Illustrated by Marina Saumell

First edition 2017
Published in the USA by Sweet Dreems Children´s Books.
Hardback ISBN: 978-0-692-93954-3

For Chris & Nick,
genuinely extraordinary young men,
I am most fortunate to be your aunt.

FOLLOW ME!

Gregory the spider
climbed up the frosty tree.

Down came the snowflakes,
pelting Gregory.

Out came the sun and dried up all the snow.

Then April wind and showers
began to blow and blow.

Gregory the spider
climbed up the Maypole.

Down came the ribbons,
roll and roll and roll!

HAPPY FATHER'S DAY!

Out came the sun
to shine upon the band.

Then Gregory the spider
spun over to the sand.

Gregory the spider
climbed up the yellow door.

Down came the leaves.
BOO!
Trick-or-treats galore!

Out came the moon
to shine upon the glen.

Then Gregory the spider
climbed up the tree again.

Follow the continuing December adventures
of Gregory and his friends,
Max and Molly Mouse in:
Merry Stirring Mice: Santa's Secret Team!

Merry Stirring Mice
Santa's Secret Team

CYNTHIA DREEMAN MEYER
Illustrations by Marina Saumell & Maria Eugenia Papeo

A note to the reader:

The name of the month is hidden in each picture. Can you find it, as well as other fun features of the months? Here are just some of the things to look for:

- [ ] A noisemaker and a snowy owl (Canadian owls visit the US in Januray).
- [ ] A stovepipe hat and a groundhog (Groundhog Day is in February).
- [ ] A clock 'springing' forward and an eagle's nest (baby eaglets hatch in March).
- [ ] Funny glasses and bears (bears come out of hibernation in April).
- [ ] A red poppy and a Pileated woodpecker (woodpeckers lay their eggs in May).
- [ ] A fairy and a fox with her kits (the best time to spot kits playing is June).
- [ ] Fireworks and 'beneficial' critters (animals/insects that help food/flowers grow in July).
- [ ] A humpback whale and baby (they can be seen all along the US east coast in August).
- [ ] A hardhat and a bluebird (bluebirds lay their last clutch of eggs in September).
- [ ] A toy ship and a brown bat (bats begin to hibernate in late October).
- [ ] A clock falling backwards and a deer (male deer have their full antlers in November).
- [ ] Mistletoe and a wolf (an ideal time to visit NJ's Lakota Wolf Preserve is December).

For a full list of the items to find in each picture,
as well as an explanation of their significance, visit:
www.sweetdreems.net

About the author

Cynthia is the author of another children's book, *Merry Stirring Mice: Santa's Secret Team.* She is also a preschool music teacher, the creator and founder of her hometown Senior Resource Center's annual Christmas Tree Festival, a black-belt in Isshinryu Karate, and an award-winning Christmas Tree decorator. She lives in New Jersey with her husband Ken; their three wonderful sons, Max, Kenny, and Gregory are all out in the world, making it a better place. They have two pups, Gracie and Scout.